SCOOBY-DOO!™

Mummy Madness

by Jesse Leon McCann

Published by Ladybird Books Ltd 2010
A Penguin Company

Penguin Books Ltd, 80 Strand,
London, WC2R 0RL, UK
Penguin Books Australia Ltd,
Camberwell, Victoria, Australia
Penguin Group (NZ), 67 Apollo Drive, Rosedale, North
Shore 0632, New Zealand
(a division of Pearson New Zealand Ltd)

www.ladybird.com

ISBN:9781409305965

10 9 8 7 6 5 4 3 2 1

Scooby-Doo and his pals from Mystery, Inc. were invited to a fancy party at a big museum in Cairo. It was to celebrate a new exhibition – the tomb of an ancient Egyptian king!

"Welcome, everyone!" announced museum curator Lotta Kayre. "Enjoy yourselves tonight . . . that is, unless King Shaggunkamen's *curse* gets you first!"

THE MYSTERIO
TREASURES OF K

SHAGGUNKAM

3

While Shaggy and Scooby guzzled food at the party, Fred, Daphne and Velma mingled in the crowd.

"*I'm* the cursed one!" artist Pierce Deere complained to Daphne. "My exhibition was cancelled, thanks to this mummy thing!"

"Humph! One shouldn't mock a curse — it might come true,"
Lord Dusty Diggs, a famous Egyptologist, told Velma. "In fact, they
shouldn't have removed King Shaggunkamen's sarcophagus from the
pyramid at all!"

"I wanted to buy King Shaggunkamen's treasures for my personal
collection," Iona Bunch, Cairo's richest resident, explained to Fred.
"But the museum wouldn't sell! 'The treasure's for everyone to enjoy!'
they said. Can you imagine?"

Shaggy dropped a spring roll, and it bounced across the floor. "Come back here, little springy-roll. Like, I'm gonna gobble you up!" Shaggy called. Scooby saw Shaggy going into an area that was off-limits. *"Ruh-oh!"*

Scooby didn't like it inside the exhibition. It was too dark and spooky. He liked it even less when a long, bony arm grabbed him from behind. *"Rooooooh!"*

It was just Shaggy! He had found some old stuff somewhere and dressed up like the ancient pharaoh.

"Like, chill out, Scoob," said Shaggy. "Look at that statue of the ol' king! He looks just like me!"

Scooby-Doo wanted to get back to the party. He didn't like tombs or ancient curses!

But Shaggy insisted they go into the sarcophagus room.
Scooby-Doo gulped when he saw where Shaggy had found his pharaoh's
outfit – in the king's ancient crypt! The cursed crypt!

Shaggy didn't notice. He was too busy admiring his reflection,
"Yep! I'm the spitting image of ol' King Shaggunkamen!"

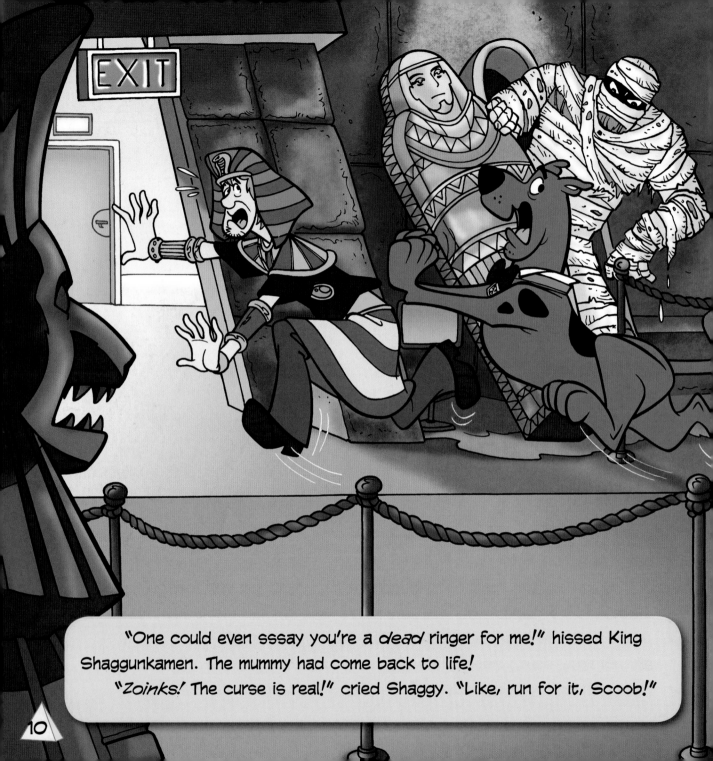

"One could even sssay you're a *dead* ringer for me!" hissed King Shaggunkamen. The mummy had come back to life!

"*Zoinks!* The curse is real!" cried Shaggy. "Like, run for it, Scoob!"

Shaggy and Scooby ran as fast as they could.

"How dare you break into my tomb!" King Shaggunkamen hissed in a high-pitched voice. "Ssseize them, my minions!"

"Relp!" Scooby yelled. "Rummies!" Just as more mummies came after them, Scooby and Shaggy found an emergency exit. A loud alarm went off when they ran through the doors. *Wee-Ooo-Wee-Ooo!*

The party-goers ran from the museum. Some people had heard the emergency alarm, and some people had seen the ghoulish mummies!

"My exhibition is ruined!" cried Lotta, the museum curator.

"Like, it's the mummy's curse!" Shaggy said.

"There's no such thing as a curse," said Fred. "I think we've got another mystery on our hands."

The Mystery, Inc. gang went back into the museum to check out the exhibition. It wasn't long before they were attacked by the growling mummies.

"Grrrwarr!"

Crash!

"*Jinkies!* Look out!" Velma hollered. "These guys have some serious anger issues!"

The gang escaped the mummies and searched King Shaggunkamen's tomb for clues.

"Look at these pearls!" Velma exclaimed. "It looks like they're from Iona Bunch's necklace."

"And there's Lord Diggs' scarf," Daphne pointed. "*Jeepers!* Is he behind all this?"

"Like, check out this groovy earring," Shaggy said. "I think I saw that grouchy artist wearing it."

"Reah! Rouchy!" Scooby nodded.

"We've got to get a close-up look at those mummies to learn more," Fred said. "Shaggy and Scooby, I'll need your help."

Shaggy and Scooby didn't like Fred's plan, but after a few Scooby Snacks, they agreed to do it. Daphne and Velma spread guacamole on Shaggy, so he looked more like the ancient King Shaggunkamen. And Scooby put on the head of a broken statue.

"Like, hey there, uh, my minions," Shaggy said to the mummies. "Like, it's me, ol' King Shaggy-carpet."

16

"I say, what's going on?" said Lord Diggs, appearing suddenly. "I slip back to look for my scarf, and the entire place goes absolutely bonkers!"

"My curssse is unleashed and you are doomed!" cried King Shaggunkamen, coming out of the shadows.

"My stars!" exclaimed Lord Diggs, as he nearly fainted from fear.

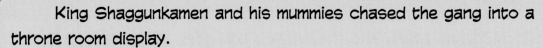

King Shaggunkamen and his mummies chased the gang into a throne room display.

"*Zoinks!* With all this guacamole on me, at least I'll be a tasty treat when I'm eaten!" Shaggy said.

Suddenly, a stone tile gave way under the gang and they fell through the floor!

"*Rooooh nooooo!*" cried Scooby.

Things went from bad to worse! The gang landed in a dusty chamber filled with dangerous snakes, spiders, and creepy, crawly insects. But they weren't the only unexpected visitors!

"Help! I fell through a hole and got stuck in this vase!" It was the artist, Pierce Deere. "Don't just stand there, get me out!"

But the gang had more important things to worry about!

"Wait a minute! These snakes are fakes," Velma said.

It was true. The snakes, spiders, and insects were all made of rubber! The gang helped Pierce get unstuck, but he thought they'd played a prank on him.

"I'm sure you think this was really funny! Well, *ha-ha*."

He left in a huff.

"*Hmm*. That urn Pierce was stuck in gives me another idea," Fred said.

Scooby-Doo and Shaggy were enlisted again to get the attention of the mummies, who chased them up some steps. Suddenly, Shaggy and Scooby turned on King Shaggunkamen and his minions and threw rubber snakes and other creepy-crawlies at them!

"Eeeek! Snakes and insects!" King Shaggunkamen screeched in a high-pitched voice. "Get them away! Get them away!"

The frightened mummies fell backwards down the stairs. Daphne, Fred and Velma caught them in Egyptian urns. Fred's plan worked!

The gang rolled the urns back to the sarcophagus room to unmask the villains.

"It's Iona Bunch and her bodyguards!" Velma exclaimed. "She must have broken her pearl necklace as she changed into her King Shaggunkamen disguise."

"I thought if I convinced everyone the treasure was really cursed, they'd sell it to me," Iona sneered. "I would have got away with it, if it hadn't been for you meddling kids and your dog!"

The next morning, the gang returned to the museum to make sure the exhibition's opening day went smoothly. Lotta Kayre, the curator, thanked the gang for all their help.

"The show is a great success and I owe it all to you and Scooby-Doo!" Lotta smiled.

"*Scooby-dooby-doo!*" cheered Scooby-Doo.